Copyright © 1994 by Nord-Süd Verlag AG, Gossau Zürich, Switzerland
First published in Switzerland under the title *Weihnachten bei Grossvater*
English translation copyright © 1994 by North-South Books Inc.

First published in the United States, Great Britain, Canada,
Australia, and New Zealand in 1994 by North-South Books,
an imprint of Nord-Süd Verlag AG, Gossau Zürich, Switzerland.

Distributed in the United States by North-South Books Inc., New York.

Library of Congress Cataloging-in-Publication Data is available.
A CIP catalogue record for this book is available from The British Library.
ISBN 1-55858-296-7 (TRADE BINDING)
ISBN 1-55858-297-5 (LIBRARY BINDING)

1 3 5 7 9 10 8 6 4 2
Printed in Belgium

Christmas with Grandfather

A STORY BY Winfried Wolf

WITH PICTURES BY Eugen Sopko

TRANSLATED BY J. ALISON JAMES

North-South Books   New York   London

IT WAS ONLY A FEW DAYS BEFORE CHRISTMAS, but Thomas was not excited. When he saw how sad his mother was, he was sure that they would never have Christmas again. He thought about how wonderful it used to be when his father was still alive. But since his father died in an accident, Thomas just couldn't believe in Christmas anymore.

Then a telegram came:

COME AND SPEND CHRISTMAS WITH ME! GRANDFATHER.

So Thomas and his mother took a train to the mountains where Grandfather lived. Silently the two of them stared out at the brown hills covered with bare trees. Gradually the landscape became white. Snow covered the houses, and the fields, and the woods.

Grandfather was at the station to greet them. He took them both in his arms and brought them to his sleigh.

"Theodore," Grandfather said, smiling to his horse, "say hello to my grandson and his mama."

Grandfather carefully tucked a blanket around the two of them, and off they went.

The sleigh skimmed over the deep snow, following the narrow road steadily uphill. The only sounds in the twilight were the soft clops of Theodore's hooves and the slipping sound of the runners on the icy crust. The horse's breath blew white clouds in the cold clear air.

The horse stopped in front of a small house wrapped up in thick snow. Inside it was warm and welcoming.

"You'll be hungry," Grandfather said. "There is food ready on the hearth. Go on and eat. I have to go out to feed the animals before it gets dark."

Thomas longed to go out in the snow and meet the animals. As if Grandfather knew what he was thinking, he turned at the door and said, "Tonight you stay inside and rest. Tomorrow you may come along to help."

Thomas rushed to the window and watched as Grandfather took Theodore into his stall. After a while he came back out, pulling a sled piled high with hay.

Thomas watched the old man trudge through the deep snow to the manger out by the woods. He piled up hay for the wild animals—a stag and a doe, and some young deer. Thomas couldn't wait for tomorrow, when he could go along.

When he turned around, he saw that his mother had set the table. He was starving, and he ran to sit down. Then all of a sudden he felt ashamed of his appetite. His father was dead, and his mother was grieving. He couldn't eat.

His mother smiled at him. She had a spoonful of soup, and said how good it was. Comforted, Thomas started eating.

"It is beautiful here," Mother said hesitantly. "I'd quite forgotten that."

Suddenly she sat upright and looked at Thomas. "It's too bad you were so young when we used to come here," she said sadly. "You were just a baby then. This is where your father grew up. This was his home. We came here often, when your grandmother was still alive.

"When she died, we didn't think Grandfather would be able to bear being out here all alone. But that was silly of us. Your grandfather is not alone; he has his woods and the animals!"

Thomas's mother told him stories about his grandmother and his grandfather, and about what his father was like when he was a little boy. She told story after story, until Thomas fell asleep.

When he woke, he was bundled up on the couch. The fire crackled and lit the dark ceiling with a flickering glow.

Mother stood quietly at the window. Outside it was already dark. Snowflakes, caught in the light of the fire, shone for a moment like frozen fireflies.

Mother turned around. "Are you awake?" she whispered. Then she smiled. "Come here, Thomas, and look!"

Outside, a fir tree blazed with burning candles.

Thomas was astonished. He didn't notice the shadowy shape trudge away from the tree of lights, towards the house. So he jumped with surprise when the door opened.

"Don't be afraid," said the smiling shadow. When the great red frozen face came into the light, Thomas realized it was his grandfather.

"Here is a Christmas tree just for you," Grandfather said. He gave Thomas a small spruce tree planted in a flowerpot. "If you plant this little tree and take good care of it, one day it will be just as big and beautiful as the tree outside."

"May I decorate it?" asked Thomas.

"Of course," said Grandfather, and he got out a couple of dusty boxes. Thomas unwrapped bright balls and delicate figures from tissue paper. The tree was so small, he had to choose carefully.

When it was decorated, Thomas lit the candles, and the three looked silently at the lights.

"Come over here," Grandfather said. "I have something for you." Thomas felt a thrill as he lifted the present onto his lap. It was so heavy. What could possibly be inside—roller skates, or a fun game…?

Impatiently Thomas ripped off the paper, and when he opened the box he was stunned. It was just an old wooden horse! There were only a few spots of faded paint left on the plump body. It was missing an ear, and it had only one eye. What a disappointment!

Then Grandfather started to talk. "That horse once belonged to your father," he said softly. "I made it for him one Christmas, when he was your age. I know it doesn't look very good, but your father loved this horse more than anything else and I'm sure he would want you to have it."

Thomas felt the disappointment melt like snow in front of the fire. He looked right into his grandfather's sad eyes. "If you help me," he said eagerly, "we can make this better again."

The two of them took the shabby wooden horse to the table and decided what they had to do to make it beautiful.

They painted and polished and fixed it up, and when they noticed that Thomas's mother had fallen asleep on the sofa, they whispered to each other until deep in the night.